JOSIE
TO THE
RESCUE

BY MARILYN SINGER

ILLUSTRATIONS BY
S. D. SCHINDLER

SCHOLASTIC PRESS • NEW YORK

LIBRARY OF CONGRESS CATALOGING-IN-PUBLICATION DATA
Singer, Marilyn.
Josie to the rescue / by Marilyn Singer.   p.   cm.
Summary: When second grader Josie overhears her
parents' concerns about the family finances, she decides
to help raise money for her soon-to-be-born baby sister.
ISBN 0-590-76339-3 (alk. paper)
[1. Helpfulness—Fiction.   2. Moneymaking
projects—Fiction.]   I. Title.
PZ7.S6172Jo   1999   [Fic]—dc21   98-23271

10 9 8 7 6 5 4 3 2 1   9/9 0/0 01 02 03
Printed in the U.S.A.   37
First edition, March 1999

The display type was set in Ablefont.
The text type was set in 15-point Goudy.
Book design by Marijka Kostiw

"Write About a Radish" on p. 6
by Karla Kuskin. Used by permission.

Many thanks to Steve Aronson, Anne Dunn, Melissa
Jenkins, Elizabeth Koehler-Pentacoff, David Lubar,
Dian Curtis Regan, and the crew at Scholastic.

To Linda
and
Yasmin
Gallop

CHAPTER ONE

Mom had eaten all the cookies.

"Oh no, not again!" said Josie.

"I know, I know. I'm bad. But I can't seem to stop eating these days." She patted her large round belly.

"You should eat things that are better for you—like salad," said Josie.

"I know, but I think this baby likes cookies," Mom replied with a guilty look.

It made Josie laugh. She didn't mind that Mom was having a baby. She already had one brother, Mickey. She liked being his older sister. It was an important job. She had to teach him a lot—the kind of stuff parents never remembered to teach. How to catch a firefly. How to jump off the back of

the couch onto the cushions without getting hurt. How much milk to put on your cornflakes so they wouldn't get too soggy too fast. She'd started keeping a list so she'd remember them all. It would take awhile before the new baby was ready to learn those things, but Josie believed in being prepared.

"I've never seen a girl as organized as Josie," her Aunt Linda liked to say. "Or as helpful. Except for my Mary Jane, of course."

Mary Jane would smile and nod like she was wearing a princess crown on her shining blonde curls and didn't want it to fall off.

Josie did not like being second to Mary Jane. She did not like the way her mother said, "Yes, Josie and Mary Jane are wonderfully helpful," instead of saying, "Why, I think Josie is even *more* helpful than Mary Jane."

"Mom, when do we start shopping for things for my new sister?" Josie asked now.

"*He* may be a *brother*," Mom said.

"I don't think so," Josie replied matter-of-factly. "So, when do we go shopping? She's going to need a lot of things—"

"Don't remind me," Mom interrupted.

But Josie went on, "Clothes and toys and diapers and a new stroller—"

"Maybe Dad can fix the old one."

"Mom, that's how it got broken in the first place!" Josie said.

"I know." Mom sighed. It seemed to Josie she was sighing a lot these days.

Late that night, Josie found out why. She woke up thirsty and went to get a glass of water. Her parents were in their room, but the door was open a little, and Josie could hear them talking.

"I don't know what we're going to do. Everything's so expensive these days. . . . Food, clothes, diapers, bottles, toys, that darn stroller . . . How are we going to afford this baby?"

"Don't worry, Alice. We'll be all right. We always make do."

"I know, Dan, but this time I'm not so sure."

Whew. Josie chewed a piece of her hair. No wonder Mom was sighing so much. Forgetting about her drink of water, she went back to her room and sat in what she called her "thinking chair." *I'll have to do something to help,* she thought. *Something wonderful. Something so fabulous Mom will stop sighing all the time. So terrific she'll know I'm a thousand times more helpful than Mary Jane.*

Josie smiled and curled up in her chair. Yes, that was a great plan! Now all she had to figure out was what that wonderful, fabulous, terrific thing would be.

CHAPTER TWO

It was too noisy for Josie to think of *any* plan, never mind a wonderful one.

There was Mickey, having a loud argument with his spoon. Mom, singing one of her favorite goofy songs about planting a radish and getting a radish instead of a brussels sprout. Dad, asking everyone if they'd seen his glasses, until Josie went and found them in the bathroom, lying on the lid of the kitty litter box.

She was glad when her best friend Flora stuck her head in the door and said, "Hurry up! Let's go!"

I'll think of something great on the way to school, Josie told herself, grabbing her backpack and scooting out the door.

But she didn't. The walk to school was noisy, too. A fire engine screamed by. A jackhammer drilled in her ears. And the rest of the time Flora wouldn't stop talking about radishes.

"Radishes!" she exclaimed. "Can you believe it? I had to write a poem about a vegetable!"

"Flora, I have to . . ." Josie tried to interrupt, but today Flora was not listening.

"There's this poet, see, who said, 'Write about a radish/Too many people write about the moon,' so Ms. Malamud said we had to write about radishes. . . ."

"Listen, Flora . . ." Josie tried again.

"It took me *forever!*" Flora went on.

Josie frowned. She loved Flora. She'd cried when she'd found out they were in different classes this year. But sometimes— like now—she wished her friend would be quiet.

"Wanna hear my poem?" Flora said. She

didn't wait for Josie to say yes. She stopped dead in the middle of the sidewalk in front of the school and struck an actor's pose. Flora planned to be either a doctor or an actor when she grew up. Josie thought maybe she could be an actor who plays a doctor on TV. "'A Radish' by Flora Fantucci. 'A radish is reddish/Except when it's deadish.'"

Josie couldn't help it. She burst out laughing.

"Thank you, thank you." Flora bowed and grinned.

Then the bell rang.

"Catch you later, elevator," Flora said.

"Be cool, swimming pool," Josie replied. With a sigh, she went off to her class.

She was barely settled in her seat when Mr. G started writing words on the blackboard:

Root
Bulb
Tuber

Mr. G was short for Mr. Groenendaal, which Artie Artelli once told Josie was a type of shepherd dog from Belgium. Josie hadn't believed him. So she'd looked it up, and he was right. From then on, to herself—and to Flora—she called the teacher Mr. Woof.

"Class," he said, "today's the first day of spring, and it's time to start thinking about our annual garden. As you know, we plant seeds that Mr. Prance, from the garden shop, is kind enough to give us. But there are other ways to get vegetables, too. We can plant bulbs—such as onions. Or we can plant tubers. . . ."

"My uncle plays the tuber," Artie Artelli called out. He did that a lot. Josie's mom said it was because he was so smart that he was bored. Josie thought she was pretty smart herself, but it didn't make *her* call out.

The class laughed. Mr. G frowned. "Potatoes are tubers," he continued. "Then there are roots. We eat the root part of lots of vegetables. For example, radishes . . ."

Josie bit back a giggle. She thought of Mom's song and Flora's poem. There was just no way of escaping radishes today.

"Mr. G, do we *have* to plant a garden this year?" asked Debbie Lemon. She called out a lot, too. But unlike Artie, she wasn't very smart. She was what Josie's mom called a "space cadet." "I don't like digging in the dirt," Debbie went on. "There are worms and things there."

"You can use the hoe, Debbie," Mr. G replied, "and don't call out. . . ."

But it was too late. Debbie had said the *w* word.

"I like worms," Artie announced. "I like to drop 'em down my uncle's tuber." He crossed his eyes at Josie. She clamped her lips tighter.

"I don't mind worms. It's slimy slugs I hate," said Armenia Jackson, wrinkling her nose.

"How about centipedes?" said Sammy Quade. He pulled out a fake rubber bug with a lot of legs and wiggled it in Armenia's direction. She squealed.

"That's enough, class!" Mr. G ordered. "The next person who calls out gets to write a report, a *long* report on worms, slugs, and centipedes."

Nobody wanted to do a long report on anything, so everyone stopped talking. Mr. G closed his eyes. Josie was sure he was counting to ten. When he opened them, he said, "Now, we were talking about radishes."

That was when Josie couldn't hold in her giggles anymore. She started to laugh and laugh and laugh. "Radishes," she roared. "Radishes!"

Mr. G was shocked. He shook his head. "Josie, that's one long report, due by Friday," he said, as if he couldn't believe it was Josie causing the ruckus.

"Yes . . . hee hee . . . Mr. G . . ." said Josie. She should have felt terrible, but she didn't. Because smack in the middle of laughing, she'd had a wonderful, fabulous, brilliant idea.

Food was expensive. But not if you grew it yourself. And that's just what she'd do. She'd plant a garden for Mom right in their backyard. She'd grow all kinds of healthy things for great big healthy salads. And the first thing she'd plant would be radishes.

CHAPTER THREE

Mr. Prance of Prance's Plants had plenty of radish seeds. Also lettuce, carrots, cucumbers, celery—everything to grow a good salad. The only problem was Josie had enough money to buy exactly one and a half packets. Flora had enough for a phone call. A family couldn't live on radishes alone.

"Mr. Prance, do you have any, uh, *cheaper* seeds?" Josie asked.

"Look in there," he replied, nodding at a basket on the counter.

LAST YEAR'S LEFTOVERS, said the sign on the basket. TWO FOR A DOLLAR. Eagerly, Josie dug into it. "Here's dandelions. And dandelions. And some more dandelions," she said, sorting through the seeds. Every

14

single packet was dandelion seeds, except for the last, which was okra, a vegetable even Josie wouldn't touch.

"Dandelions?" Flora read over her shoulder. "Those don't look like dandelions."

Josie stared at the picture on the packets. Instead of those bright yellow flowers with the fluffy white seeds she and Flora used to puff away, there was a salad bowl full of long green leaves. "Maybe it's a different kind of dandelion," she said. "A lettuce-dandelion."

"A lettelion," Flora declared. Then she pretended to be someone's mother: "Finish your lettelion, dear. It's full of vitamins and those other things, whatever they call 'em."

"You think so?" asked Josie.

"Think so what?"

"Think lettelions are good for you?"

"Sure," said Flora. "Look at the picture. It's a salad, right?"

Josie nodded. "Okay then, lend me your quarter."

"My quarter? But what if I have to make an emergency phone call?"

"We're five minutes from my house. What kind of emergency could you have five minutes from my house?"

"More emergencies happen near your home than anywhere else," Flora said, imitating a TV announcer.

"*Please*, Flora. I need twenty-five more cents to buy these seeds."

"Oh, all right," Flora gave in. "But if I fall over a crack in the sidewalk and break my arm, if I get discovered by a big producer and have to call Mom to tell her I'm on my way to Hollywood, if I swallow my spit wrong and start choking, you're gonna have to *beg* a quarter off someone so I can call home."

"You won't be able to call *anyone* if you're *choking*," said Josie.

Flora bopped her on the head with a seed packet and gave her the quarter.

Josie bought one packet of radish seeds and two of dandelion. Mr. Prance threw in a third one of dandelion for free.

"Wow! Thanks, Mr. Prance!" said Josie.

"Sure, sure." He flicked a hand at her.

"Now we can go plant the garden." Josie beamed as she and Flora left the shop.

"*We?*" Flora replied.

"You will help me, won't you?"

Flora cocked her head. "Can I wear your big straw hat and overalls?"

"Why?"

"Because if I'm gonna act like a farmer, I wanna look like one," Flora said.

"Okay, you can wear them," said Josie. "So, will you help?"

"Sure, sure," said Flora, flicking her hand just like Mr. Prance.

Josie laughed and bopped her over the head with the bag of seeds.

CHAPTER FOUR

Mickey was playing Poodle. He had a pair of long ears fitted over his curly brown hair and a plastic dog nose on his face, and he was crawling around the house, sniffing everything. And barking. Loudly. It was driving Mom crazy.

"Mickey, please stop that. Now," she was saying when Josie and Flora walked in.

"Hi, Trickey-Mickey," Josie greeted her brother.

"Hi, Mickster," said Flora, who liked little kids a lot.

"I'm Mookie," he said, naming the dog down the street. He sniffed their shoes, threw back his head, and howled.

"That's it! Do that again and you'll *really* be in the doghouse!" Mom yelled. She rubbed her head as if it hurt.

"Mickey . . . uh . . . *Mookie*, you come with us," Josie said. "We've got some stuff to do in the backyard." She didn't plan to tell Mom what it was till they finished. She wanted it to be a good surprise.

"Ruff!" Mickey said, nodding his head.

"Oh, thank you, thank you," Mom said, as Josie led him away gently by one ear.

"You wait here," Josie told her brother outside her room while Flora changed into Josie's overalls and hat. Then the three of them went outside.

"So, where d'ya want ta plant the crops?" Flora said, chomping on a piece of grass and talking in what she thought was a farmer's voice.

Josie studied her big backyard. Some parts were already planted with bushes, grass, and trees. But there were a couple of bare spots that Josie thought would be just right for vegetables.

"There," she said, pointing to one of them. She went and got two small shovels and a hoe.

"Okay, Mookie, you ready to dig?" she asked.

"Woof!" he barked.

"I'll take the hoe," said Flora.

"How come?" asked Josie, who wanted the hoe herself.

"It goes better with my outfit."

"You mean *my* outfit," said Josie. "You just happen to be wearing it." But she handed Flora the hoe.

It had been a warm winter, but the ground was still a little hard. Flora had to chop and chop away at the top few inches of soil until she got tired. "Are you sure we should be gardening this early?" she said.

"Of course I'm sure," said Josie, although she wasn't. Then she took over the hoeing.

Mickey sat at the far end of the patch, using his hands like paws to dig in the dirt she loosened.

"Okay, we're ready to plant," Josie said, finishing a furrow. "I'll do the radishes. You start on the lettelions."

Flora didn't argue. But there were so many lettelion seeds, Josie soon had to help her. They planted them close together, but still had a whole packet and a half left when they were done. Should they start another patch? Josie stretched and yawned. She was tired already. Gardening was not easy work.

Then Mickey jumped up. "Look! Look!" he shouted. His pants and his face were smeared with dirt.

"Look! Look" he shouted, totally forgetting his dog act. He had something in his hands. "Look what I found!" He waved a fistful of bulbs.

Josie hurried over and stared at them. "Onions!" she exclaimed. "You found onions!" Here they'd been planting slow-growing seeds and they already had food in their garden! Amazing! But how had the onions gotten there? Maybe the last people who owned the house had planted them and Mom and Dad just hadn't noticed before.

"What's going on?" Flora came over.

"Look at this," said Josie. "We found onions!"

"*I* found them," said Mickey proudly.

Flora stared at the bulbs with a puzzled expression. "Are you sure those are onions? They're kind of small."

"Maybe they're not full-grown yet," Josie said. "But that's okay. Baby veggies are even *more* nutritious than big ones," she said. She was pretty sure she'd heard that sometime. "We'll dig up some more, put them in a nice basket, and give them to Mom. She makes great onion soup."

There were a lot of bulbs in Mickey's

patch. It was even harder digging them up than planting the seeds. Flora grumbled a lot, and Josie had to keep telling herself over and over that the work was worth it because she was doing something terrific. Something Mary Jane would never *think* to do. When they had enough, Josie got a basket from the garage and arranged the onions inside. She finished just as Mom came into the yard.

"Look who's here," Mom said.

Josie looked. There were Aunt Linda and Mary Jane. Perfect! Josie almost laughed.

"What have you been doing back here?" Mom asked.

"It's a surprise," Josie said, holding the basket behind her back. She grinned at Flora, then at Mom.

"Show her, show her!" Mickey jumped up and down.

"Two surprises really. Surprise Number

One—this! We planted vegetables. *Healthy* vegetables for a salad!"

Mom blinked. "There? You planted them there? That's my flower bed."

Josie frowned. Mom did not seem pleased.

"What did you plant?" she asked.

"Radishes," Josie told her. "And these." She held out an empty seed packet.

"*Dandelions?* You planted dandelions?" Her mother's voice rose.

"Not regular dandelions," Flora put in. "Lettelions."

"There's no such thing," said Aunt Linda. "All dandelions are the same. You know that, don't you, Mary Jane?"

"Yes, Mummy," Mary Jane said. It was what English kids called their mothers. Josie thought it might sound okay if Mary Jane were English, but she wasn't.

"I don't believe it!" said Flora.

"It's true. All dandelions are the same, and they're all *weeds*." Mary Jane smiled, carefully nodding her head.

Flora smiled back, mimicking her.

Josie bit her lip.

"Maybe they won't come up—it's too early for planting. But you'll probably be lucky, and they will." Mary Jane beamed.

"Show her what I found! Show her!" Mickey shouted. He didn't know anything about dandelions and he didn't care.

"Huh? Oh! Oh, yes," Josie said. Maybe the onions would make up for the dandelions. "We found these. Right in our garden!" She held out the basket. "Onions! For onion soup!"

"Oh, no," said mother. She looked pale. "Oh, no, no."

"What's wrong?" Josie asked, her voice quivering.

Aunt Linda looked into the basket. "Josie, dear. I'm afraid those aren't onions."

"They're n-not? Wh-what are they?" Josie asked, her voice getting smaller and shakier.

"Mary Jane, can you tell her?"

Josie's cousin picked up one bulb. "Yes, I can. They're tulips."

"Tulips?" said Josie.

"I didn't think they looked like onions," said Flora.

Josie poked her.

"Tulips are a flower," said Mary Jane.

"I know that," said Josie.

"And they come from bulbs."

"I know that, too."

Mary Jane smiled at Josie like she didn't believe it.

"I think I need to lie down a bit," Mom said, rubbing her head even harder than she'd done before.

"You do that," said Aunt Linda. "I'll make us some tea. . . . Mary Jane, why don't you give Josie a lesson in gardening? Mary

Jane's very good at gardening, aren't you, dear?"

"Yes. I am," Mary Jane agreed.

Aunt Linda led Josie's mother away. Trying not to cry, Josie put down the basket.

"Guess you don't know much about gardening," Mary Jane said. "So we'll have to start at the beginning." She pointed to the big maple tree. "This is a tree," she said, and laughed. It wasn't a nice laugh. "And this"—she bent down and picked up a handful of soil—"is dirt."

"This," said Flora, taking the big straw hat off her head, "is what gardeners wear to keep off the sun." She squashed it down on Mary Jane's head.

"Don't do that! You'll mess up my hair!" yelled Mary Jane.

Flora turned to grin at Josie.

But Josie was running out of the yard.

CHAPTER FIVE

"Hello, I'm the oh-so-helpful Mary Jane, but you can just call me Full 'cause I'm so *full* of myself. . . ." Flora strutted up and down the sidewalk, trying to make Josie laugh.

It wasn't working.

"She put the tulips back in the ground," Josie said glumly. "She said they might bloom after all. And she offered to come pull out the dandelions when they come up."

"I'm soooo full of help I just want to hug myself." Flora struck a haughty pose and batted her eyes at Josie.

Josie just shook her head. "Come on, Flora, or we'll be late for school."

Flora turned down her mouth. She hated it when she couldn't get Josie to smile. "Is your mom still mad at you?" she asked.

"No. She said she wasn't really mad, period. She said she knew I was just trying to help."

"Well, you were," said Flora.

"But I messed up," said Josie. "How will I ever be as helpful as Mary Jane?"

"There are other ways to be helpful," Flora answered. But she didn't say what they were.

Then they reached the school.

"See you around, said the mound." Flora waved.

"Hang loose, said the noose." Josie gave a mournful sigh.

Throughout most of the morning she still felt sad until Mr. G told them they were going to get a chance to let off some steam.

"We're going to visit a sauna?" Artie called out.

"What's a sauna?" asked Debbie.

Louisa Reinstein raised her hand. Mr. G called on her. "It's a small room which is very hot where you go to sweat."

"Eww," said Armenia. "Why would somebody go some place to sweat?"

"I don't like when I sweat," said Debbie.

"I don't like when you sweat either," Sammy said.

Josie rolled her eyes. Why couldn't they stop goofing around? She sure needed to let off some steam and she wanted to hear how they were going to do it. Would they stomp around the room, shouting? That was how Flora let off steam. Would they bake bread, punching the dough really hard? That was the way Josie's mom let off steam. Or would they do what her dad did, which was to put on loud music and sing?

"That's enough silliness," said Mr G, as if he'd read her mind. "Remember how last month we wrote letters to authors telling them how good their books were? Well, today we're going to write letters of *complaint*."

Huh? Josie frowned. She couldn't imagine how writing a letter would let off even a wisp of steam.

"You're going to pick something you don't like about this school and complain about it in a letter."

Louisa raised her hand. "Who will we send the letters to?"

"To the principal," said Mr. G.

"Ooh!" "Wow!" "Yikes!" Josie's classmates exclaimed.

"Great!" said Josie.

Mr. G heard her. "It looks as if Josie has plenty to complain about."

You said it, Josie thought. But suddenly she got worried. Quickly she raised her hand.

"Yes, Josie?" Mr. G called on her.

"Won't we get in trouble?" she asked.

"No. The principal is expecting your letters. . . ."

"Great!" Josie repeated.

Mr. G nodded. "Now, let me show you
how to start and then you'll have half an
hour to finish them."

Twenty-five minutes later Josie was
staring at a piece of paper. It said, "Dear
Ms. Markell, I am writing because I don't
like . . ." and nothing else. Another piece of
paper listed all the stuff she didn't like. The
way the art teacher called her Josephine
instead of Josie. Sitting next to Sammy
Quade. And especially being in a different
class from Flora. But she wasn't sure that
Ms. Markell could change any of those
things. She wanted to pick the right thing
to complain about. Something that Ms.
Markell might actually fix.

One thing stuck in her mind, but it was
too embarrassing to write about. It was the

school's toilet paper. It was stiff, scratchy, nasty stuff. Josie hated it, and so did everybody else. *If I complained, Ms. Markell could get different paper*, Josie thought. But she just couldn't make her hand write those two words. Weren't there another two words for it? She was trying to remember.

"Okay, class, time to hand in your letters," said Mr. G.

"No, wait . . ." Josie whispered. She grabbed her pen. "I don't like being in a different class from my best friend, Flora," she wrote. Even if Ms. Markell couldn't do anything about that now, at least it felt good to complain about it. Then, the rest came to her. ". . . and I don't like the <u>bathroom</u> <u>tissue</u>," she finished, underlining both words. It wasn't her neatest letter, but it would have to do.

Before she could cross anything out, she folded the paper in half and handed it in.

Then she raised her hand.

"Yes, Josie?"

"Mr. G, you're not going to read these out loud, are you?"

"No, I won't," he replied.

Whew, she sighed to herself.

"She must have complained about the toilet paper," said Sammy.

The class giggled.

Josie turned red. "You'll be sorry, Sammy Quade," she murmured. Now that was really letting off steam—right out of her ears!

CHAPTER SIX

"Toilet paper, toilet paper, toilet paper," Sammy sang, walking past Josie with his lunch tray.

"Toilet paperrrr," echoed his friend Louie Bonano.

"Shoo! Go away!" Flora ordered them, in her most queenly voice, as if they were nothing but cats. She'd only just heard what had happened to Josie in class.

Josie sat there, not looking at Sammy and Louie. But her face was still red.

"Look, she's blushing!" said Louie.

"Don't blush, Josie," said Debbie, sitting next to Flora. "Everybody has to go to the bathroom."

Flora shook her head. Josie hunched further down in her seat.

Sammy and Louie poked each other and sat down at the other end of the table.

"Listen, you're right about the toilet paper. It *is* crummy." Artie plopped himself right next to Josie.

"Who asked *you* to join us?" said Flora.

"I didn't know I needed an invitation," said Artie, sounding more like eighteen than eight.

"You wouldn't get one," said Flora.

Artie ignored her. "But you shouldn't write to the principal," he went on to Josie. "You should write to the company. That's what my dad does. All the time. He doesn't like the way some soap smells, he complains to the company. He thinks some cereal tastes yucky, he writes to the company. Works every time."

"What do you mean it works?" asked Armenia, munching a large peanut butter and carrot sandwich. Armenia was small and ordinary-looking. Her sandwiches were large and weird. "You mean the company changes the smell or the taste?"

"No, but they send him a free box of the stuff."

"A free box? Why would he want a free box if he didn't like it to begin with?" asked Flora.

Artie shrugged. "He says it's the principle of the thing."

"You just said *not* to write to the principal," Debbie said, confused.

"That's a different principle."

"Your dad writes to a different principal?"

"Like, uh, excuse me, but, like what planet are you from?" Flora asked her in a dumb girl voice.

"Earth," said Debbie.

Everyone laughed except Josie. She was thinking. "You mean if I wrote to Dampers Diapers or Softie Wipes or Boomer Bottles and said their stuff stunk, they'd send me a whole box for free?" she said.

"Sure, most of the time. If you complain good enough," said Artie.

"What do you mean, 'complain good enough'?"

"You can't just say 'Dear Mr. Damper, your diapers stink.'"

"Diapers always stink," said Debbie. She wasn't making a joke, but everybody laughed again, except, this time, Artie. He'd been enjoying having everyone's attention and he wanted it back.

He raised his voice. "You have to say something like, 'Dear Mr. Damper, you claim that your diapers don't leak. But they do.'"

"Hmmm," said Josie. "Or 'Dear Ms. Boomer, your bottles weren't supposed to break, but they did.'"

"Right," said Artie.

"Or 'Dear Mr. Softie, is your last name really Wipe?'" said Debbie.

Armenia laughed so hard juice came out of her nose. Flora laughed so hard she fell off her chair.

At the other end of the table, Sammy and Louie started throwing hot dog roll bullets at them.

"Hmmm," Josie said again, ignoring all of them. She had an idea. A big idea. The trouble was it meant lying. Josie hated to lie — even a little. *Well,* she said to herself, *maybe it isn't lying. Maybe Dampers Diapers aren't so great. Maybe they could be better. A lot better. And cheaper, too. So Mom and Dad could afford them. I mean, it's bad to lie, but what about if you're not lying for yourself, but for your family? What if a little lie would help my family a lot? More than Mary Jane could ever help hers.* She squinted at Artie. "Would they send you *more* than one box?"

"I don't think so. Not to the same person," Artie answered.

"But what if you needed, really needed more than one box? Like what if it were for a good cause?"

Artie squinted back at her, curiously. "Well, I guess you could get your friends to write, too."

"You think my friends would help even if it meant lying a little?"

"Well, yeah, I suppose if it's for a good cause. . . ."

"Hmmm," said Josie. She looked around the table. It would be tricky. For one thing, she couldn't let Mom find out about it. For another, she and Flora were planning to play Sleeping Beauty that afternoon. Oh, well, Flora was her best friend. She'd understand.

Josie took a deep breath. "How would you all like to get together after school. . . ."

"Can't," said Armenia.

"Sure," said Debbie.

"Okay," said Artie.

Flora stared at her, shocked.

But she was even more shocked when Josie added, "Good. We can all walk together. It won't take long to get there. Flora's house is right nearby."

CHAPTER SEVEN

"See, I knew you girls would make more friends," Flora's mother said loudly, opening the door wide for them when they arrived. She was convinced that Josie and Flora would have a great time being in different classes.

Uh oh, Josie thought. She liked Flora's mom. But she had what Josie's dad called a "foghorn voice" and sometimes she said the wrong thing. And then Flora would get bugged and she'd say an embarrassing thing back.

Josie was afraid that was about to happen. And it did.

"They're not my friends. They're Josie's,"

Flora said, loud enough for everyone to hear.

They're not my friends, either, Josie wanted to say. But that would've been too rude. Besides, friends helped you out. Artie and Debbie were going to help out. If they weren't friends, what were they? Partners, like they had on school projects? Assistants, like Uncle Steve had in his office? *Acquaintances*, that funny word Josie didn't like because Mary Jane used it? Josie didn't know—and that bothered her. She liked things to be clear.

"Well, good for you, Josie!" said Flora's mother. "Maybe soon you'll make some friends of your own, too, Flora."

Flora was about to say some other embarrassing thing, so Josie grabbed her hand. "Come on, Flora. Let's go to your room. It's so pretty."

Flora gave Josie a look. "Pretty?" she sniffed.

Uh oh, thought Josie again. There was no way Flora's room could be called pretty. Interesting. Different. But not pretty.

"You know what I mean—it's special," Josie corrected herself.

Flora sniffed again, but she did lead Josie, Artie, and Debbie downstairs.

Flora's room was big. There was a desk on one side and a bed on the other with a quilt covered in green and purple roses. At the end was a stage, an actual stage, with a microphone and a trunk of costumes. On the walls were posters of people and movies. Next door was Flora's own bathroom. Next door to that was the furnace.

"You sleep in the *basement?*" said Debbie.

"No, I sleep in the *bed,*" Flora retorted.

"A *flower* bed," said Artie, pointing to the crazy quilt.

"Ha ha," said Flora, not laughing.

After her tulip/onion adventure, the last thing Josie wanted to think about was flower beds of any kind. "Um, could we please work on those letters now?" she begged.

Flora gave in. "Okay," she said. She went to her desk and took out her nicest stationery—the one with the dancing bananas on the top.

"Don't you have anything plainer?" asked Artie.

"What's wrong with this?" Flora stuck it in his face.

"It doesn't look like stuff a grown-up would use," he said.

Flora humphed, but she took out plain white paper and envelopes.

"And we should use scrap paper first," Artie said. "Then when the letters are perfect, we can copy them onto the real stationery."

"Mine will be perfect right away," said Flora, with her hands on her hips.

"*Nobody's* is perfect right away."

"Oh, yeah? How do you know?"

"Because I know everything." Artie grinned.

Josie frowned. Flora and Artie reminded her of a film she'd seen about fighting lobsters, each of them waving their claws, not backing down. "That's it," she declared. "If you two don't cut it out, we won't get anything done!"

Flora and Artie went quiet. Then Debbie held up a piece of stationery she'd already written on. "Does *diaper* have one *b* or two?" she said.

Artie snorted.

Flora went and got the scrap paper.

They worked for a long time. Debbie's letters were neat, but had a lot of spelling mistakes. Flora's had few spelling mistakes, but they were messy. Josie's just didn't sound right.

"You can't say, 'Please, please, please

send me a free box of your diapers,'" said Artie. "You have to *make* them want to send you a box."

"How?" Josie asked.

"I told you how. You have to tell them their product's bad."

"I did that," said Josie. She had, too, even though she didn't feel so great writing it.

"And you have to make them feel their product messed up your baby. Or babies. It would be even better if there was more than one."

"Like the Mitchums," said Debbie.

"Right." Artie nodded. The Mitchums had triplets.

"Hmmm," said Josie. What if she pretended she had triplets? Wait—what if she pretended she had ten babies, twenty babies, a whole *nursery* of babies to care for? What if she said she ran a day-care center?

They needed more than a box of diapers there. They needed a shopping cart full. Brilliant! The idea was brilliant!

Quickly she tore up the old letter and started writing a new one. Then she stopped. This wasn't a little lie, but a huge one. It made her stomach feel funny. *But it would* really *help Mom and Dad,* she told herself. *And when I'm old and rich, I'll buy a ton of Dampers diapers and I'll give* them *to a day-care center.* She took a deep breath, picked up her pen, and wrote fast before she could change her mind.

"Done!" Flora sang, waving *her* letter in the air. "And no mistakes." She glared at Artie.

"I'm done, too," said Debbie. This time she'd misspelled her name, but they all figured nobody would notice.

"Wait, wait," said Josie, her pen flying across the page. "Okay! Look at this."

She handed her letter to Artie.

"Wow!" he said, after he read it. "I couldn't have done better myself."

"What? Let me see," Flora demanded. She was annoyed that Josie hadn't shown it to her first. But when she read it, she whistled. "Whoo. That *is* great! Especially the part about the diapers leaking and messing up the new rug during playtime."

Finally Debbie read it. "It's very good," she agreed.

"Thanks," said Josie. She knew Mary Jane would never come up with anything so clever. Not in a million years.

"It's very good," Debbie repeated. "But I don't think the day-care center has a new rug."

"Josie's does," said Artie.

Everyone laughed.

CHAPTER EIGHT

Flora was the first to get a box of diapers. She was so excited she called Josie on the phone. "It worked!" she shouted. "They really sent a whole box!"

"Well, I guess they wouldn't send just one diaper, would they?" Josie giggled. She was still feeling a little guilty about lying, but she let excitement push that feeling away. She knew she'd be even more excited when her diapers came. Artie said they'd probably send her a whole case!

Flora brought her box over while Josie's mom was out shopping and Josie's dad was busy in the basement, trying to fix the old baby stroller again.

"Hurry, I don't want Dad to see it," Josie

said. "Let's hide it in my closet. I want it to be a surprise."

Dad didn't see it, but Mickey did. "Diapers?" he said. "I don't wear those anymore."

"I do," said Flora. "Wha wha wha," she pretended to be a baby.

"She does?" Mickey was wide-eyed.

"She's just kidding," said Josie.

"Wha wha wha," Flora faked crying.

"Do you drink from a bottle, too?" asked Mickey.

"Sure," said Flora. She picked up an imaginary bottle and drank from it.

Mickey watched, fascinated. "Is that milk or juice?"

"Both," said Flora.

"Ewww," said both Josie and Mickey, which made them all laugh.

Artie got his box next. He brought it right over to Josie's without calling first. Dad was at work, but Mom was doing the laundry. Luckily Josie herself answered the door. She practically pushed Artie into her room.

"What's the problem?" he asked.

"I don't want Mom to see. It's going to be a surprise," Josie explained for a second time.

"But what happens if they deliver *your* case when you're not here?"

Josie frowned. She hadn't thought of that. "I don't know."

"You could talk to Pete the Mailman. Tell him to hold it at the post office for you."

"That's a good idea," Josie said. Artie really did know an awful lot.

Pete was easy to find. Josie saw him every day on the way home from school.

"No problem," Pete told her. "I'll hold it for you and I'll tell you when it's there."

But the next day, and the day after, it still hadn't arrived.

Debbie's box did, though. On Thursday morning she brought it to school and put it on Josie's desk.

"Boy, Josie," Sammy called out, "you must *really* hate the toilet paper here!"

Everyone cracked up.

Josie turned redder than the sweater Mr. G was wearing when he entered the room.

He took one look at the box of diapers, another at Josie's face, and he said, "I'm not even going to ask. Just put it in the coat closet, Josie."

The class watched her carry it to the closet and giggled. They giggled when she walked back to her desk, too. She never thought she'd be so happy to have a spelling test. But today she was. It was the only thing that shut everyone up.

But only for a while. At lunch Sammy and Louie teased her like crazy.

"Isn't it time to change your diapers?" Sammy said.

"Yeah. P.U." said Louie, holding his nose.

"They're not for her," Debbie tried to be helpful and explain.

It only made things worse.

"Who are they for then? Her friend Flora?" said Louie.

Flora didn't kid with Sammy and Louie the way she had with Mickey. "They're for *you*," she said. "Because if anybody's a baby, you are!"

"Oooh, arrggh." Sammy clapped his hand over his heart as if Flora had shot him. Then he and Louie laughed.

Josie pulled the neck of her turtleneck up to her nose and wished she could pull it over her whole head. She wondered if Mary Jane ever got so embarrassed while she was being helpful. She hoped so.

She was glad when lunch was over, gladder still when the last bell of the day rang. She practically ran out of class.

"Come on, Flora," she said, grabbing her friend's hand as she came out of her classroom door. "Let's go before Sammy and Louie see us."

"I'm not scared of them," said Flora, but she hurried anyway.

They raced to Josie's house.

"Whew," Josie said when they got there. *Safe*, she thought. *No more trouble today.* To be sure, she stashed the box of diapers behind the bushes. *I'll get them later when everybody's asleep*, Josie thought. With a grin she opened the door and walked into the living room.

And there was her mother with her hands on her hips.

"Josephine Jellico," she said. Her eyes blazed as if they might light the fireplace. "Just what is the meaning of all this?"

There on the floor, piled so high they almost touched the ceiling, were one hundred and sixteen cardboard cases filled with one thousand, one hundred and sixty boxes of Dampers Guaranteed Leakproof Diapers.

CHAPTER NINE

"Wow," Flora exclaimed. "Your baby sister will have enough diapers to last till she's potty trained!"

Josie poked her. Her letter couldn't have worked that well. Something had gone wrong, and now her mother was furious. She thought about pretending she didn't know anything about the diapers. But she knew she couldn't. She could lie to the diaper company, but not to her mother.

"What on earth is this, Josie?" Mom asked.

"A surprise?" Josie tried.

"It's that all right." Josie could tell she was trying not to yell. "Now tell me just what you did to get Dampers Diapers to deliver all these cases to our house—and I know you did it because your name is on the delivery slip."

Slowly, Josie did. It felt worse than having ten cavities filled at the dentist.

Mom gave up trying not to yell. "Josie!" she exploded. "You mean you lied about running a day-care center?"

Josie hung her head.

"She just pretended to run a day-care center, Ms. Jellico," Flora said. "Like acting."

"Acting isn't pretending to be someone else in a *letter*, is it, Flora?"

"Well, maybe not," she had to admit.

"And you lied about their product being bad, too," Mom went on angrily to Josie.

Josie's head hung lower.

"Well, it could be bad," Flora said.

"And it could be good. You and Josie don't really know, do you? Do you, Josie?"

Josie's head was so low she wished she

could just hide it under the rug. "I just wanted to help," she said miserably. "I know it was lying and lying's bad, but what if it's to do something good, like helping your family?"

Her mother shook her head. "It's still lying and it's still bad." Then her voice got a little more gentle. "We're not *that* broke, Josie. We can afford diapers." But Josie wasn't sure she believed it.

Then Mom cleared her throat and Josie knew she was about to pass sentence, like a judge. "Now you have to call the company and tell them the truth. You have to give the diapers back."

Josie was horrified. "I can't do that!" she said. She heard Flora sigh, but she didn't dare to look at her.

"Yes, you can—and you will." Mom was firm.

Josie bit her lip. "Couldn't I get punished some other way?"

"Fixing your mistakes isn't a punishment."

But to Josie it sure felt that way. "All right," she said with a sigh.

Mom got the number and dialed. Then she put Josie on the phone. The woman on the other end seemed confused. Josie had to repeat the story three times. Finally, she hung up.

"They're going to pick up the diapers tomorrow," she said.

"Good." Mom patted her shoulder.

"And they said it was a computer mistake. They meant to send only sixteen boxes."

"I see," said Mom, sucking in her lips. For the first time that afternoon, Josie thought she was trying not to laugh. Mom patted her shoulder. "I know that was hard, but I'll bet you feel better for telling the truth."

"I guess so," Josie said. But the truth was she didn't feel better at all. She felt worse.

Instead of being more helpful than Mary Jane, she felt less helpful than her baby sister, who wasn't even born yet!

"Don't worry," Flora whispered in her ear. "We'll think of another plan—one where you don't have to pretend."

Josie shook her head. The last thing she wanted to think about was another helpful idea. She said good-bye to Flora and went to her room. She lay down on her bed and fell asleep. She dreamed she was a good fairy who made everyone's wishes come true. It was a great dream till Mary Jane came along with a bigger wand. Everyone thought Mary Jane was better than Josie, even in her dreams.

Josie woke up and sighed. Flora was right. They *would* have to think of another plan. But what? Josie didn't have a clue.

CHAPTER TEN

"Look, Josie," said Mickey. "No drips." He held up his ice cream cone. Josie had shown him how to lick around the edges before the ice cream melted.

"Good for you," she said, poking at her ice cream sundae. She, Mickey, and Flora were sitting at a table in The Big Scoop. Mom and Flora's mother were sitting at another. Usually it made Josie feel good and grown-up to have her own table. But today nothing made her feel happy.

"Calling all girls named Josie. Calling all girls named Josie," Flora said, making a bullhorn out of her hands. "Cheer up immediately. I repeat, cheer up immediately."

Josie smiled a little, but she didn't really cheer up.

"Are you kids finished?" asked Flora's mother.

"Yes," Flora said.

"Why Josie," said Mom, "you didn't even touch your sundae."

"She touched it. She just didn't eat it," said Mickey, which made everyone but Josie laugh.

Next door to the ice cream parlor was the Comfy Baby store. It sold carriages, strollers, and baby furniture. Today there was a big banner in the window. CONTEST! it said. WIN THIS WONDERFUL STROLLER!

A stroller! Just what her baby sister would need. "Look at that!" Josie said, feeling enthusiastic for the first time that day. She thought Mom would be eager, too, but she and Flora's mother were talking to Ms. Jonas, whom they'd just run into on the street. Ms. Jonas was the leader of the Girl Scout troop. Josie liked being a Girl Scout, except when it came to selling cookies. She wasn't any good at it. Not like Flora was. Josie knew Ms. Jonas was going to ask how many boxes she'd sold this week. Josie didn't want to tell her she hadn't sold any. So she grabbed Flora's hand and went over to the store window, with Mickey following.

Underneath the banner was a group of photographs. Six were of grown-ups and six were of little kids. "'Contest rules,'" Josie read out loud. "'Match these people with their baby pictures. Enter by May first. Winner to be announced on Mother's Day.'"

"Ha!" said Flora. "That's easy!"

"Easy?" said Josie, staring at the pictures. It didn't look so easy to her.

"Sure. That's Mr. Prance—and that's Mr.

Prance as a little boy," said Flora. "It looks just like him."

"You're right," said Josie. "It does look just like him."

"And that's Dr. Shepperson." Flora pointed to another baby picture. She had no clothes on and was lying on a rug. "I've seen that picture a hundred times."

Mickey started to giggle. Josie did, too. She'd seen that picture as well. Dr. Shepperson, whom just about all the kids in town went to, kept it in her office to make everyone laugh.

"But what about the rest of the pictures?" Josie asked.

"Well, that's Mr. Romero, who owns this store. There's only one other picture of a little boy, so it must be him," said Flora.

"And them?" Josie pointed to the other three adult photos. One was Mrs. Racktree, who sold antiques out of her house, just down the street. Another was their principal, Ms. Markell. The third looked really familiar. It took Josie and Flora a moment to realize it was Sammy Quade's mother.

"Well, that one's simple," said Flora. "We just ask Sammy which baby is his mom."

Josie stared at her. Yesterday on the way home they had avoided Sammy and Louie. But not today. Today Sammy had teased Josie after school until some poor cat covered in what looked like flour ran by them. "That's terrible! Who'd do that to a cat?" Sammy said, truly upset, which surprised Josie. And then he'd run after it.

"Are you kidding?" Josie said to Flora. "Number one, I don't want to ask Sammy Quade anything. Number two, he probably wouldn't tell me anyway."

"Well then, we'll just have to figure out the other two," said Flora. "The one left over will be Mrs. Quade."

"How? How will we figure them out?"

Flora squinted, thinking hard. "I bet they have baby pictures in their houses."

"We can't just go to their houses and ask to see their baby pictures," said Josie.

"I guess not," said Flora, stumped.

Josie sighed. She really wanted to win that contest. Her new sister needed that stroller. If she won it, nobody but nobody would doubt that she was more helpful than Mary Jane. She stared at the pictures and chewed her hair. What if they had a *reason* for going to their houses? What if they were selling something? Something like . . . Girl Scout cookies?

It wouldn't be lying, Josie thought. *Not at all. But it would be cheating, wouldn't it? Well, maybe not. If the pictures happened to be there. And I sort of just happened to notice them. . . .*

"Flora, you haven't gone cookie-selling outside your block yet, have you?"

"No," said Flora. "Why?"

Josie turned and looked at their mothers.

Ms. Jonas was still there. She waved them over. "So Josie, how many boxes of cookies did you sell this week?" she asked, just as Josie knew she would.

"I haven't sold any," Josie answered truthfully. "But I'm going to try harder. And I think today might just be my lucky day."

CHAPTER ELEVEN

Josie couldn't believe it. It was too easy. Mrs. Racktree actually *wanted* to buy cookies. And she *wanted* Josie and Flora to come inside her house. And right there, on the mantelpiece, was the old picture of her and her sisters when they were kids. What hadn't been so easy was leaving because Mrs. Racktree liked to talk. A lot. But Josie didn't mind that much. She knew that she and Flora had to go to Ms. Markell's house next.

Josie had never been in the principal's office, much less her house. It made her nervous.

"Don't worry," said Flora, who had been

in Ms. Markell's office a few times. "It's not like we're doing anything wrong."

"I know," said Josie, but somehow it still felt that way.

The principal's house was too far to walk to. So they had to get Flora's mother to give them a ride.

"Don't be long," Flora's mother said. "I have to go to the gym and work off that ice cream sundae I ate so I can eat another one tomorrow."

"We won't be," said Flora.

"We hope," muttered Josie, and she rang the bell.

"Why, Josie and Flora, what a surprise!" said Ms. Markell when she opened the door.

Josie was surprised, too, that the principal knew her name.

"What can I do for you?" she asked.

"Well . . . well . . ." Josie stuttered. She'd

suddenly forgotten what they were there for.

"Cookies!" said Flora. "We're selling delicious, nutritious, Girl Scout cookies. May we come in and show you our fabulous selection? We have three new flavors."

Josie grinned. It was fun to see Flora acting just like a salesperson. No wonder she was so good at selling cookies.

"That's wonderful," said the principal.

Josie smiled again. She was sure Ms. Markell was going to invite them in.

Instead the principal said, "But I'm afraid I can't buy any. You see, if I bought them from you, I'd have to buy them from every Girl Scout in our school. So I just give a donation to the Girl Scouts instead."

"Oh, uh, well . . ." Josie stammered again. Well, that was it. Her great plan had failed. Bye-bye, stroller. She pictured her baby sister bumping along in the old broken one while Mary Jane smirked, and she sighed.

Then Flora said, "We understand. We've got plenty of other people to try. So many people we'll be doing this for hours. And hours. So do you think before we try *all* those other people we could use your bathroom, Ms. Markell?"

Josie let out a little squeak. Had her best friend really just asked the principal what Josie thought she'd asked?

"Why, certainly," said Ms. Markell, and she let them into her house.

The bathroom was right next to Ms. Markell's bedroom. Ms. Markell led them to it and went down to the kitchen.

"Okay, you stand guard," Flora said.

"What?" Josie gasped. "We can't . . ."

"You want to win this contest or not?" said Flora.

"But . . ."

"Then stand guard!" Flora ordered.

Josie didn't have time to say no. Flora had already headed for the bedroom. Josie stood there in the hall, her stomach flipping and flopping until Flora came back.

"Well?" she demanded.

Flora shook her head. "Nothing," she said. "No pictures anywhere."

"Girls," called the principal, "is everything all right up there?"

"Fine, Ms. Markell," Flora called.

"We'd better go right now," whispered Josie.

Flora nodded.

They hurried downstairs, thanked the principal, and left.

"Well, we tried," said Flora.

Josie frowned. She still wanted to win that contest, and now there was only one way. They'd have to go to Sammy Quade's house after all.

"I guess we'll have to go to Sammy

Quade's house after all," said Flora, reading her mind.

Josie's frown got bigger. "Yes, but I have to do something else first."

"What?" asked Flora.

Josie looked down at her feet. "Go to the bathroom," she said.

"Oh no," Flora replied, and she tried not to laugh.

CHAPTER TWELVE

"Three chocolate mints and two peanut butter. No, *two* chocolate mints and *three* peanut butter," said Mrs. Quade. She looked worried. She always looked worried. Josie thought if she had a kid like Sammy Quade, she'd look worried, too. "No, wait," Mrs. Quade went on. "Let me look at that cookie list again. . . ."

Josie tapped her foot on the floor. Flora gave her a warning look and she stopped. Across Mrs. Quade's living room were bookshelves. On those shelves Josie could see two big photo albums. She felt as though she'd been staring at the spines of those albums forever while Mrs. Quade tried and tried to make up her mind.

Josie was trying to make up her mind, too. Should she peek at the albums or not? Well, she thought, they were on a bookshelf. It was okay to look at things on a bookshelf, right? It wasn't the same as poking around in somebody's dresser drawers or going into her bedroom. She swallowed hard, thinking about Ms. Markell and what would have happened if they'd gotten caught. *Never mind,* she told herself. *We didn't—and we didn't see any pictures, either, and this is my last chance.* She tapped her foot again and made up her mind. She *had* to peek. But how on earth could she with Mrs. Quade in the room?

"Oh dear," said Mrs. Quade, staring at the cookie flier. "This is so hard. They all look so good. It's too bad Sammy's not here. He'd help me choose."

Josie didn't think it was bad at all. She hoped Sammy would stay away until she

84

and Flora were gone. She rolled her eyes at Flora.

"Was that your phone?" Flora asked. Josie quickly turned her head away. She knew Flora was trying to get Mrs. Quade to leave the room.

It didn't work. "I don't think so," Sammy's mother said.

Josie swallowed a sigh. It seemed as though she was just going to have to guess which kid picture belonged to which grown-up. Maybe she'd win the contest that way. But probably she wouldn't. She could see the brand-new baby stroller rolling farther and farther away.

Then the phone rang for real. "Oh dear," said Mrs. Quade. "Don't go away. I'll be right back."

"Don't worry," said Flora. "We'll be right here."

As soon as Sammy's mother left the room, Josie and Flora jumped up and grabbed the photo albums. They flipped quickly through them.

"This one's all recent pictures," said Flora.

"So's this one," said Josie, feeling frantic. She looked over the shelves. Lying flat on top of a dictionary was a third photo album, thinner and more worn than the others.

Flora saw it, too, and she pulled it off the shelf.

"Be careful," said Josie. The book looked like it was about to fall apart.

"This is it!" Flora said, excitedly, handing Josie the book. "Look. Here she is." Then she started to imitate Mrs. Quade. "I mean, I think that's her. Or could it be this one? Or maybe it's the one in the chocolate mint-colored hat. Oh dear, I wish Sammy were here to help me choose."

"Oh yeah? Then this is your lucky day," a familiar voice said.

Josie slammed the album shut and stuck it back on the shelf.

But it was too late. Standing there in the doorway was Sammy Quade. And it was clear from his grin that he knew just what she and Flora had been doing.

"So, who shall I tell first, Mom or Mr. Romero?" he said.

"Tell them what?" Flora challenged. "We weren't cheating."

"No? What do you call it?"

"Research," Flora replied.

Then Mrs. Quade came back into the room.

"Hey Mom, you know that picture of you in the Comfy Baby contest? Weren't you wearing Dampers Diapers?" Sammy said slyly.

Josie bit her lip.

Mrs. Quade didn't answer. Josie wasn't sure she'd even heard him. She was looking more worried than ever. "I can't believe it, Sammy. I know you can be naughty sometimes, but honestly, how could you throw flour on Mr. Rose's cat?"

"I didn't throw any flour on any cat," Sammy declared. "I'd never do that!"

"Mr. Rose says he saw you chasing it down the street."

"I was trying to catch it to wipe it off." He looked at Josie. You were there, his eyes said. You saw.

Josie stared back with a little smile. I told you you'd be sorry, it said.

Mrs. Quade threw up her hands. "Sammy, Sammy, what am I going to do with you? You know how I feel about lying. No TV for two weeks."

"But . . ."

"And no baseball, either."

"But . . ."

"And no but's," said Mrs. Quade.

Sammy's face turned red. He looked at Josie once more. His lips quivered. Embarrassed, he lowered his head.

Josie stopped smiling. She thought revenge would be fun. It wasn't. "Mrs. Quade, Sammy isn't lying," she said quietly.

Sammy raised his head.

Blinking, Mrs. Quade turned. She'd forgotten Josie and Flora were there. "How do you know?" she said.

"Sammy, Flora, and I, we saw the cat run by and it was already covered with flour and Sammy felt sorry for it."

"Did you see who did it?"

"No, but it wasn't Sammy," Josie replied. She stared at him.

He stared back.

"Well, all right. I'll call Mr. Rose and tell him," said Mrs. Quade. She started to leave the room, but then she turned back. "Sammy, did you ask me something before? Something about diapers?"

Still staring at Josie, Sammy shook his head. "Nope," he replied. "Not me."

"Okay," said his mother, walking out.

Josie took a big breath. "We're even," she said.

"Don't count on it," Sammy mumbled. But from the way he was shuffling his feet, Josie knew she could.

CHAPTER THIRTEEN

Mom and Dad were taking forever to eat breakfast.

"This is delicious, Josie! What a great Mother's Day surprise!" one or the other of them would say after every bite.

Wait till they see the real *surprise,* Josie thought.

"Josie, you're a good cook," said Mickey. "Can I have some more pancakes?"

"Sure." She sighed. At this rate they'd never get out of there.

But at last Dad pushed his plate away. "Whew! I couldn't eat another bite!"

"You couldn't?" Josie perked up.

"Nope."

"I could," said Mom.

"Really?" Josie sighed again.

"*Not*." Mom laughed.

"Great!" Josie whisked away both their plates. "Hurry and get dressed," she said, sounding like her mother. "We've got to be there at noon."

"Be where?" asked Mom.

"You'll see," Josie said.

"Here we are," Josie said half an hour later when they arrived at the Comfy Baby store. Flora and her mother were already there.

"Isn't it exciting?" Flora said. "Look at all the people!"

Josie glanced around. There *were* a lot of people. The contest was more popular than she'd thought. She saw Artie Artelli and his mom, Armenia and her aunt, Debbie and her oldest sister, who had just had a baby last month. Had they all entered the contest? *Well, so what*, Josie thought. She knew *her* answers were right.

"Oh, it's the *photo contest!*" said Mom. "I was going to enter this, but I couldn't figure out who was who." She looked at Josie. "You mean you did?"

Josie nodded.

"Wow!" Mom was impressed. "All of them?"

"All of them," Josie told her. "I did some . . . research. Flora helped." She looked at her friend, dancing in a little circle.

"Then you're gonna win, Josie," said Mickey.

"I think so," she said, crossing her fingers. Then she turned and saw Aunt Linda and Mary Jane coming toward them.

"Well, look who's here!" said Aunt Linda.

"Don't tell me you entered this contest, too," said Mom.

"I didn't. Mary Jane did. She wants to win that stroller just for you."

Josie felt her stomach give a squeeze. She stared at her cousin. Mary Jane was smiling like she'd already done just that.

"Oh yeah?" Flora couldn't help asking. "How'd you figure out all the answers?"

"I'm not going to give away my secrets," Mary Jane replied, cutting her eyes away. It made her look guilty.

"Because you don't *have* any to *give* away," Flora said.

"That's what you think," said Mary Jane, still not looking at Josie.

Josie couldn't tell if she meant it or not, but it bugged her.

Then someone said, "Here we go!" From Mr. Romero's back room came all six of the grown-ups in the photos. Mr. Romero himself came last, holding an envelope in his hand.

"All right," he said. "This is how we're going to do it. One by one, each of us will stand by his or her baby picture. I'll go first."

Slowly, to make it dramatic, each of them did. And each time Flora would count, "One right, two right, three right . . ."

Around them, people yelled, "Ooh. Oh. Phooey. Hooray!" depending on how well they did with their guesses.

"Six right!" Flora said at last.

"Good going!" said her mother.

"Yay!" Josie's mom cheered.

Grinning, Josie looked across the room. Sammy Quade was watching her. He gave her a quick thumbs-up. It made her grin even more. *I did it. I really did it.*

But then her dad said, "Wait. What if someone else got all the answers right?"

Josie hadn't thought about that. Would Mr. Romero give away more than one stroller?

"In this envelope," he said, "is the name of the contest winner. This person got all the answers right . . ."

Josie sucked in her breath. Flora squealed.

". . . along with fifteen other people."

Josie let out her breath with a gasp. Flora squealed again, but this time it wasn't a happy sound. Fifteen? How? Did they go to Mrs. Racktree's and Ms. Markell's and Mrs. Quade's houses, too?

"The final winner was selected at random from those sixteen people. . . ." Mr. Romero went on.

At random? What did that mean? She looked at Flora, who frowned and shrugged, then at her dad. "It means they pulled a name out of a hat," he said.

"What!" Josie yelled.

"Shh," said Debbie Lemon's aunt. She had her fingers crossed.

Oh no, no! Josie couldn't believe it. She must have the right answers, too! She looked around the room and saw several other people who were smiling excitedly and holding up *their* crossed fingers, hoping they'd won.

Josie shut her eyes. She didn't want to look at them. They couldn't have won. They just couldn't have. She heard Mr. Romero open the envelope, heard him say, "And the winner is . . ."

Me, Josie said silently. Me, me, me.

"Mary Jane Borman!"

Josie wasn't sure whose scream was louder—her cousin's or her own.

"You did it! You did it!" shouted Aunt Linda. She hugged Mary Jane, Josie's mother, and then Josie. "Isn't your cousin terrific?" she said to Josie. "The most thoughtful, generous, helpful girl in the world!"

Josie looked at her cousin, smiling like a dog that had just stolen somebody else's sirloin steak. "I hate you, Mary Jane!" she cried. "I hate you!" And she ran out of the store.

CHAPTER FOURTEEN

"May I come in?" asked Mom, standing in the doorway. "Or should I say *all* the way in." She looked down at her big belly, which was sticking into Josie's room, and smiled.

"Okay," Josie answered. She was sitting on her bed twisting white and black pipe cleaners into a person—one of her "piple," as Dad called them. Sometimes she made them when she was happy. Other times, like now, she made them when she really needed to cheer up.

"What's that one called?" Mom asked.

"Skunk Man," said Josie.

Mom laughed. "Mickey will love that."

"I guess." Mickey was crazy about Josie's

piple. He could watch her work on them for hours.

"So will your new sister or brother," said Mom. "Think of how helpful that will be when I need to take a nap."

Josie looked at her. "But not as helpful as Mary Jane," she said sadly. "I can never, ever be as helpful as Mary Jane. Even when I lie and cheat."

"Cheat?" said her mother.

Josie sighed. "When I was selling cookies, I looked at people's baby photos," she said.

"That was your research?" Mom said.

Josie gave Skunk Man's arms another twist and, blinking back tears, waited for Mom to scold her again.

But instead her mother lowered herself onto the bed next to Josie. "Oof," she said. "Just call me graceful."

Another time Josie might have laughed, but not now.

"You know, I always wanted to be more helpful than someone, too," Mom said. "Can you guess who?"

Josie shook her head.

"No? Well then, I'll tell you. It's Aunt Linda."

"Aunt Linda!" Josie was surprised—and she wasn't.

"Yep. The whole time we were growing up I wanted to be more helpful, more smart, more *everything* than she was. I'll let you in on a big secret. Sometimes I *still* feel that way. And I hate it!"

Josie's forehead wrinkled. "So what do you do then?"

"I punch some dough good and hard and tell myself I've got better things to do with my time than worry about outdoing Linda."

Josie nodded, but she looked unhappy. "But Mom, don't *you* care whether or not I'm more helpful than Mary Jane?"

Mom picked up Skunk Man and danced him along Josie's arm. "I think you're more helpful than you even know. Who else would make sure Dad doesn't have to buy a new pair of glasses every few weeks? Who else could save me having to do laundry every time Mickey eats an ice cream cone? And who else would hide a box of Dampers Diapers behind the lilac bush and leave them in the rain?"

"Oh no!" Josie's hand flew to her mouth. She'd forgotten all about that box of diapers.

"Don't worry," said Mom, trying to look serious. "They really *are* leakproof." Then she started to laugh.

Josie tried not to, but she couldn't help it.

When they both stopped, Mom said, "Flora's coming over for dinner."

"Great!" said Josie.

"So is Mary Jane."

Josie's face fell. "Do I have to apologize?"

"Do you want to?"

"No—but I guess I will." She sighed.

"Good. So will Mary Jane," said Mom.

Josie blinked. "For what?"

"For cheating at the contest. Aunt Linda told me she overheard your cousin bragging to a friend that she saw you go into Comfy Baby to enter it. She went in after you left, found your entry blank on top of the pile while Mr. Romero wasn't looking, and copied it. Aunt Linda made her return the stroller to Mr. Romero so someone else can win it."

"*What?* But how'd she know I was right?"

"It seems Mary Jane thinks you're always right—except when it comes to tulips."

"She does?" Josie squeaked.

"Yep. But we won't tell her she's wrong, will we?"

"Nope," said Josie, with an amazed smile. "Our lips are sealed."

She and her mother zipped their lips and, hand in hand, they went to the kitchen to punch some dough good and hard before dinner.